"Kris Davis's new children's books, *Seek and Find Hiking and What Can You See on a Hike?* are superb resources for parents who want to expose their children to the great outdoors".

- Scott Marchant, author of Hiking Idaho Guidebooks

"Kris created a unique book to help parents make hiking fun and educational for children. The guides are loaded with tips and information that turn an average walk into a joyous adventure for your children."

- Kurt Koontz, author of A Million Steps and Practice

"*What Can You See on a Hike?* encourages kids to get outside, sharing practical skills for planning, education and games while observing nature. An excellent book that kids and parents can both enjoy!"

- The Ward Family Christina and Co, Keller Williams Realty

Copyright © 2024

Kris Davis

eBook ISBN: 978-1-965064-10-8

Paperback ISBN: 978-1-965064-11-5

All Rights Reserved. Any unauthorized reprint or use of this material is strictly prohibited. No part of this book may be reproduced or transmitted in any form or by any means, electronic or mechanical, including photocopying, recording, or by any information storage and retrieval system without express written permission from the author.

All reasonable attempts have been made to verify the accuracy of the information provided in this publication. Nevertheless, the author assumes no responsibility for any errors and/or omissions.

What Can You See on a Hike?

Kris Davis

Contents

Dedication 1

Information for Parents 2

Hiking Checklist For Kids 4

Trail Etiquette 5

Children's Reading Pages 6

Checklist 16

Hiking Journal 17

Activities to do While Hiking 18

Remembering Your Hike 19

High Frequency Word Practice 20

Safety Tips 22

Acknowledgments 24

About the Author 25

Photo Credits 26

Dedication

I would like to dedicate this book to my two daughters, Cassie and Cecelia, who have been lifelong hikers and wonderful supporters of their mama.

Information for Parents

Throughout my 33 years of teaching elementary children, I have gained considerable knowledge and experience with teaching children to read. My idea for this book was not only to get kids excited about hiking and practicing reading but also to educate parents/caregivers on ways to build foundational reading and mathematical skills. This book is for ages 4-6.

A very effective method for learning to read is implementing repeated readings using one-to-one correspondence. This means the child will point under each word as it is read. The progression of repeated readings can look like this:

1. The adult models the reading of the sentence first while holding the child's finger or pointer under each word read.
2. The child can try reading while the adult holds the finger or pointer.
3. The child can try reading and pointing on his/her own as the sentence moves from left to right. An effective reading strategy is using the picture clue to help read the word.

One finger can make an easily accessible pointer, but other pointy objects can add more excitement and creativity. Examples of these could be using a pencil, pen, crayon, or marker. Fun erasers added to the top of an unsharpened pencil make great pointers. A craft stick could be decorated, and a foam shape could be glued at the top, such as a tree or leaf cutout. Simply pick up a small stick from the path and use it to point to the words.

Remember to praise the beginning reader for all the efforts made. I will never forget the day 2 students went into the cubbies of my classroom, and I heard one boy say another, "I just learned to read!" with pure excitement and squeals in his voice. It melted my heart. Learning to read can, however, be challenging. Therefore, lots of repeated readings of simple, decodable text (simple words that can be sounded out), along with high frequency word practice, are the keys to building these foundational reading skills. Here's a quick suggestion to help aid in the word practice, use a stick to write words in the dirt, such as the ones in the book: I, a, can, see. Reread the children's pages many times prior to hiking.

Another concept that I wanted to bring to light is how much vocabulary and mathematical thinking can be developed while trekking down the trail. Simply comparing two objects discovered along the path can spark conversation and build these skills.

Rocks: which is lighter or heavier

Sticks: which is longer or shorter

Leaves: which is pointed or rounded

Bark: which is smooth or rough

Flowers: which smell sweet, musky, or stinky

You could also line several objects up in order of length, height, or weight (small, smaller, smallest or heavy, heavier, heaviest). See if you can find two different objects that are equal in size or weight. Another idea is using one-to-one correspondence with counting objects. Children need to learn how to count by touching each object as they say the numbers in sequential order. To stay accurate, it is beneficial to slide each object over one at a time to avoid counting an object more than once or missing one. It's amazing how much new vocabulary and mathematical skills can be acquired through these simple activities.

Hiking Checklist For Kids

Here is a list of items that your child may want to carry in his/her backpack. You might want to carry some items, alleviating weight off your child's back.

- Backpack
- What Can You See on a Hike?
- Pointer for reading
- Water Bottle
- Snacks (something new/special is fun)
- Sunglasses
- Bug Spray
- Sunblock
- Sunhat
- Baggie for trash
- Toilet paper/shovel/baggie for toilet paper
- Wipes/hand sanitizer
- Simple First Aid Kit
- Bandana (dip in water and wrap around neck to keep cool or sit on if there's a sappy log)
- Binoculars
- Magnifying glass
- Walkie talkies
- Trekking poles
- Camera
- Paper/Pencil/Notebook

Make sure your child has hiking boots, hiking socks, and possibly water shoes if there is a river crossing.

Please help your child understand that it is not necessary to find all the items in the book. Hopefully, there will be more hikes in the future. If the area you are hiking in doesn't have the exact kind of animal or plant, just use the pictures as a reference. Have fun exploring nature.

Trail Etiquette

- Review any rules posted on or by trail signs.
- Be respectful and friendly to other hikers on the trail (say hello, don't play loud music).
- Step aside for uphill hikers so they can keep their momentum.
- Don't hike on muddy trails. It leaves a lasting impression.
- Avoid approaching or feeding wildlife. It is unsafe for humans and animals.
- Stay on the trail as much as possible to avoid stepping on vegetation or causing erosion by taking shortcuts.
- Pack it in/pack it out: do not litter or leave food. If you find litter, pick it up and put it in the trash baggie you brought to throw away when at home.
- Don't build/destroy rock cairns. They are navigational tools for hikers following the trail.
- If you need to go to the bathroom, find a spot 200 feet from the trail or water source. Pack out toilet paper and bury solid waste. Try to avoid stepping on vegetation.
- Please use your best judgment when taking rocks and flowers home. Do not take from state or national parks.

Children's Reading Pages

I can see a trail sign.

I can see a bird.

I can see a flower.

I can see a caterpillar.

I can see a waterfall.

I can see a butterfly.

I can see a mushroom.

I can see moss on rocks.

I can see a bridge.

I can see a firepit.

Checklist

	trail sign	☐		butterfly	☐
	bird	☐		mushroom	☐
	flower	☐		moss	☐
	caterpillar	☐		bridge	☐
	waterfall	☐		firepit	☐

Hiking Journal

Date_____ Trail_____ Something else I saw_____	Date_____ Trail_____ Something else I saw_____
Date_____ Trail_____ Something else I saw_____	Date_____ Trail_____ Something else I saw_____
Date_____ Trail_____ Something else I saw_____	Date_____ Trail_____ Something else I saw_____

Record your hiking trips and anything else fun you saw. A picture can be drawn in the box.

Activities to do While Hiking

- 'I Spy' Game: Say, "I spy with my little eye something that is ____?" The child tries to guess what you see.

- ABC Spying: Find something that starts with the letter a, then b, and so on.

- 20 Questions: Hide something in your backpack, and the child can ask 20 different yes/no questions to see if it can be figured out before you get to 20 questions.

- Hide and Seek: One person runs up the trail and hides, being careful not to go off the trail too much. The rest of the hikers go seeking after that person. You could also hide a stuffed animal or other object along the trail.

- Follow the Leader: One person leads the group, walking different ways while all hikers follow behind copying the leader's movements. You can try skipping, jumping, flapping arms, lunging, waving, just being silly.

- Sing songs or recite nursery rhymes such as "Jack and Jill" or "Little Bo Peep."

- Take pictures of your hike with your phone, or you could purchase a kid's camera on Amazon.

- Count how many different colored objects can be found (3 red, 2 yellow, etc.)

- Tell stories like fairy tales such as "The Three Little Pigs" and "Jack and the Beanstalk," or make up your own. Each person can have a turn telling part of the story.

Remembering Your Hike

- Create your own storybook: Take 3-4 pieces of paper, fold them in half, and staple them along the edge. Record events from the hike, making each sentence as easy to read as possible. For example: We hiked. I can see a _____. I can see a _____. I can see a _____. I like hiking. We had fun. You can draw pictures to match the words or glue in the photos of pictures you took while hiking.

- Pick your favorite rock to take home. At the bottom, write the name of the hike and the date with a permanent marker. As rocks are collected from different hikes, a rock cairn could be built in your house or yard. The rock could be painted with designs or messages.

- Collect some leaves and place them in between 2 sheets of wax paper. Place a thin towel over the wax paper and iron the 2 sheets together. You can tape or hang the leaf collection in the window. It's especially beautiful in the fall with all the different colored leaves found.

- Frame pictures of your hike or glue 4 craft sticks together to make a frame. Scrapbook the hike using a program such as Shutterfly or crafting your own pages.

- Collect some sticks and make different creations such as teepees, rafts, mobiles, and weavings. Pinterest has some great ideas.

High Frequency Word Practice

- Write the book's high frequency words on index cards. Or have your child write them.

- Make a duplicate set of index cards to play a memory game. Turn all 12 cards over and take turns picking up 2 cards to see if they match. If so, keep them and pick 2 more. If not, replace cards in the same spot they came from. The winner has the most pairs at the end of the game.

- Practice writing words with crayons, markers, pencil, pen, watercolor paints, or sidewalk chalk.

- Manipulate pipe cleaners or playdough (rolling out like a snake) to form the letters of the words.

- Flatten playdough or clay with a rolling pin and write the words on top pressing in with a pencil.

- Spell the words using magnets on a fridge or cookie sheet.

- Write the word in a sentence to practice reading.

I	a
can	see
on	(child's name)

Safety Tips

Apply sunscreen and insect repellant. Wear a hat to shade your face and sunglasses to protect your eyes from the sun.

Blisters: Wear hiking shoes with hard soles, that are a half size bigger than your feet, along with a pair of wool blend socks that are long enough to cover your upper ankles. This will help to avoid blisters. Try not to get your socks wet. If a big blister occurs, wash with soapy water or alcohol swab. Take a sterile needle or safety pin and puncture the blister at the base. Soak up the liquid with gauze and apply antibiotic ointment and a bandage.

Minor Cuts and Puncture Wounds: Wash the wound with soap and water. If still bleeding, press on it with a clean cloth (bandana) until the bleeding stops. Apply antibacterial ointment and a clean bandage.

Dehydration: Drink plenty of water before you even start your hike. Take frequent water breaks during your hike (perhaps every 20 minutes). Sports drink powders can make water more enticing to drink and provide electrolytes. If someone has symptoms of being thirsty, having a headache, feeling tired or muscle weakness, then take a rest in a cool place with elevated feet, drink lots of fluids, and eat a salty snack.

Poison Ivy: The sap from these 3 leafed plants causes a serious rash with red itchy bumps. Wash skin that was in contact with soapy water. Apply calamine lotion or creams with menthol. Take an oral antihistamine such as Benadryl. Poison oak looks like poison ivy. A popular saying is, "Leaves of three, let them be."

Ticks: Wearing light weight long sleeves and pants can deter ticks from getting onto your skin. Check your body and hair for ticks after your walk. If you find one stuck to the skin, use a tweezer to grasp the head or mouth of the tick. Pull straight up not twisting or rocking it from side to side. Clean the bite area with an alcohol pad or soap and water. Put the live tick in a plastic bag, alcohol, flush it down the toilet or wrap it tightly in tape.

Snakes: To avoid encounters with snakes, walk on the trail with a trekking pole or walking stick. Tap the ground as you walk and the vibration made will be sensed by the snake and it will get out of your way or let you know it is there (rattling tail from a rattlesnake). If you see one on the trail, keep a 6-10 foot distance from it, walking backwards if needed and wait for it to move away. Don't poke it or try to move it. If bitten, try to remain calm to keep the venom from spreading. Be able to describe the the color and shape of the snake. Clean the bite with soap and water. Seek medical attention as soon as possible. Be aware of what type of snakes inhabit the area you will be hiking.

Acknowledgments

I would like to thank several people for their support and encouragement during the writing process. Thank you to my husband, Mike Davis, for encouraging me to follow my dream of becoming a children's author. Thank you to my wonderful friends for being my cheerleaders: Teresa Carter, for helping me to edit the grammar; Diane Dodge, who pushed me to get started and helped me with the cover of the book; and Rebecca Auston, for sharing in the passion of becoming a children's author and helping me with ideas during the process. I'd also like to thank my project manager, Brian Wilson, at Wiley Publishing, for being patient with me and all my questions.

About the Author

Kris Davis lives in Boise, Idaho with her husband, Mike, and 2 Australian Shepards, Ruby and Indi. She taught elementary aged students for 33 years before retiring. She has been an avid hiker her whole adult life but became a backpacker in 2015. Kris and her friend, Patty, conquered 3 sections of the Pacific Crest Trail in Oregon and Washington. This is a picture of her backpacking near Twin Lakes on the Alice Toxaway Loop in Stanley, ID. Many of the photos in the book were taken by Kris. She has a great desire to motivate children to want to hike and explore nature. But she also wants to continue to educate parents on foundational reading and math skills.

Photo Credits

Cover: Keitma - stock.adobe.com

Page 7 - Bird: Hummingbird Art - stock.adobe.com

Page 8 - Flower: sticker2you - stock.adobe.com

Page 9 - Caterpillar: Vasiliy Koval - stock.adobe.com

Page 12 - Mushroom: Danila Shtantsov - stock.adobe.com

Page 23 - Poison Ivy: Bill - stock.adobe.com

Tick: Vitalii Hulai - stock.adobe.com

Seek and Find Hiking

When your child is a little older and can read more fluently, he/she is ready for my 2nd book, "Seek and Find Hiking". It is written in the same format as this book but has many more challenging activities with harder reading pages designed for ages 7-9. You will be surprised at some of the interesting facts on each page.

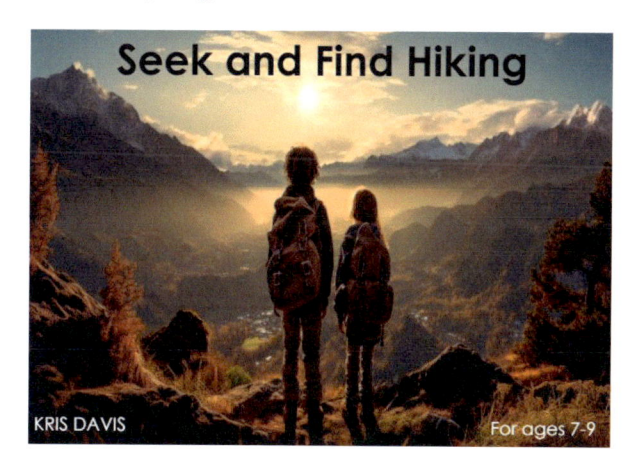

I will seek and find a slug.
What does it look like?

You can order from Amazon or my website at

www.kristinanndavis.com

Made in United States
Troutdale, OR
03/27/2025